COMING CLEAN

NICK WARBURTON

Illustrated by Toni Goffe

dingles & company

First published in the United States of America in 2008 by
dingles & company
P.O. Box 508
Sea Girt, New Jersey 08750

First Printing

Website: www.dingles.com
E-mail: info@dingles.com

Library of Congress Catalog Card Number
2007906271

ISBN
978-1-59646-876-4 (library binding)
978-1-59646-877-1 (paperback)

Coming Clean
Text © Nick Warburton, 1995
This U.S. edition of *Coming Clean*, originally published in English in
1995, is published by arrangement with Oxford University Press.

The moral rights of the author have been asserted.
Database right Oxford University Press (maker).

Printed in China

Old Baggy-Pants

Derek and Janey were eating their lunch and talking about Mr. Such's pants. Mr. Such was their teacher, and he wore the exact same pants to school every day, day in and day out.

"They're so crumpled and baggy," Janey said.

"And grubby and heavy," said
Derek.

"Like a pair of old dish-cloths."

"And he wears them all the time."

"I don't think he's got any others."

"Old Baggy-Pants, that's what he
is," Derek added, between bites of his
lunch.

"I wish he'd get some new ones,"
Janey sighed.

At that moment, Old Baggy-Pants himself came into the lunchroom. Janey's mouth fell open, and Derek could see the food all mashed up inside her mouth!

"What's up?" he said.

Janey blinked and pointed. There was Mr. Such in a brand new suit. A spotless white suit without a crease in it. Everyone in the lunchroom stopped eating and stared at him.

"Okay, everyone," said Mr. Such, his face a bit red. 'Keep on eating."

5

"Wow!" said Derek, leaning across his plate. "He looks so different."

"He looks sharp," said Janey firmly. "And about time, too."

Later that afternoon, Janey's class trooped into the gym for P.E.

"I like the suit, sir," Janey told Mr. Such as they filed in.

"Thank you, Janey. It's for Parents' Evening, really."

"Parents' Evening?"

"Yes, I have to look my best for that, don't I?"

"But that's not till Monday, Mr. Such," Derek said.

"I know that, Derek. I'm just getting used to it."

While they were talking, Mrs. Venn came out of the kitchen holding a bowl of pudding in her hands.

She was so shocked to see Mr. Such in his bright new suit that she gave a little jump. "Oh my gosh!" she cried.

She grabbed a curtain to steady herself. The pudding flew into the air, straight for Mr. Such.

Derek saw it coming and stepped in the way. The pudding wobbled through the air and flopped against Derek's gym shirt. Everyone became silent. Derek stood there, looking sad and stunned. And he was covered with cold pudding.

"Good move, Derek!" said Mr. Such. "You've saved my brand new suit."

Derek tried to smile, but by then the custard was oozing into his gym shorts!

After recess, Mr. Such changed back into his dish-cloth pants.

"Please keep clear of this," he said, hanging his new suit on the closet door. "Be sure not to go near it!"

A Wonderful Green Color

The last class of the day was art. They had to paint interesting faces. Janey was doing a monster. She put bloodshot veins in his eyes, a bolt through his neck, and green stuff coming out of his nose. She was pleased with the green stuff, but she'd mixed up too much. She asked Derek if he wanted some.

"I don't need any green stuff, Janey," he said. "I'm doing a soccer player."

"Well, he could have green stuff coming out of his nose, couldn't he?" she said.

"No," said Derek. "He couldn't."

"You could use it as background. Like grass."

"I'm not having my soccer star running around on green stuff from a monster's nose, thank you," said Derek.

He nudged Janey's elbow, and green stuff spilled over the desk.

He tried to stop it from trickling onto the floor.

Then he reached behind him and rubbed his hands on a towel. Except that it wasn't a towel.

"Uh-oh," he said quietly. "What have I done?"

Janey could see what had happened. Derek had wiped his hands on Mr. Such's new pants.

"Now you've done it," she said. "Old Baggy-Pants will hit the ceiling when he sees this."

Mr. Such was on the other side of the room. He looked up and smiled at them.

"Are you doing okay, you two?" he asked.

"Yes, thank you, sir," said Janey brightly.

She didn't dare tell him the truth.

She grabbed some paper and started to rub at the green spots.

"What do you think you're doing?" said Derek. "you're making them worse. They're twice as big now."

They were. Janey looked at Derek and thought hard.

"There's only one thing to do now," she said.

"What's that?"

"Put them back on the hanger. Then we can clean them up after school."

When Mr. Such came over to look at their pictures, the suit was still swinging slightly on the cupboard door.

"Oh," he said. "I love that shade of green, Janey. That's a wonderful color."

14

After the last class Mr. Such hung around for ages and would not leave the kids on their own. They stacked chairs as slowly as chairs have ever been stacked. Then, at last, he wandered off to the teacher's lounge.

Derek darted over to the sink and turned on the water. Janey grabbed the pants and flung them to him from across the room. He caught them and plunged them into the sink. He grabbed a plastic bottle and squirted it right on the pants.

"What are you doing?" Janey yelled.

"I'm putting on hand soap," said
Derek. "That'll get the stains out."

"That's not hand soap, Derek. That's
glue."

Almost at once they heard Mr. Such
outside the door. He came in wearing
his jacket and cycling clips. Derek and
Janey stood side by side in front of the
sink.

"Oh," said Mr. Such. "Are you still
here?"

"Nearly finished, sir," Janey said,
and tried to smile.

"Well, it looks tidy to me. I should go
home now."

He went over to the jacket on the
cupboard door.

"Don't!" said Derek.

"Don't what?"

"Don't take the suit."

"Why not?"

"Because… because…"

"Because you might get it dirty,"
Janey said. "It'll be safer if you leave it
here. Won't it, Derek?"

Derek nodded. Mr. Such looked
puzzled. His hand was still halfway to
the jacket.

"It might fall off your bike," Janey
added, "and land on a heap of garbage
or something."

Mr. Such lowered his hand.

"Well," he said. "you might be right.
I don't want any more accidents."

When he'd gone, they put the pants
in a plastic bag and smuggled them off
to Derek's house.

They threw the pants in the kitchen
sink and covered them with
hot water and laundry powder. They
scrubbed them with a stiff brush, a bar
of soap, and some kind of wiry thing.
The water foamed into a pile of
bubbles as high as their elbows.

"Is it working?" Janey asked.

Derek flapped the bubbles
out of the way and looked into
the sink.

"Still green," he groaned.

"They squirted dishwashing liquid,
furniture polish, and floor cleaner in
the sink, but they didn't work, either.

"Maybe we should bash them around
like a washing machine," said Derek.

So they ran outside and bashed the
pants up and down on the sidewalk in
front of Derek's house. But that just
picked up more dirt. And Janey
thought the pants were beginning to
shrink.

"There's only one thing to do now,"
she said.

"What's that?"

"We'll have to take them
to the dry cleaners."

The Hero

The next day was Saturday. Derek and Janey caught the first bus into town. The pants sat on the seat between them, rolled up tight in a plastic bag. Janey could hardly stand to look at them.

They waited until the dry cleaners was empty and then marched in. Janey smiled at the woman and the woman smiled back.

"The pants, Derek," Janey said.

"What about them?"

"Hand them over."

"I can't."

"Why not?"

"Because you've got them."

"No I haven't. You have."

For a moment or two they stood there staring at each other. Then Derek blinked and said in a quiet voice, "Janey, they're still on the bus."

Three hours later, tired from their long walk, they arrived at the bus station. They walked up and down until they saw their bus. It was parked in a corner, with two feet sticking out from under it.

"Excuse me," Janey said to the feet, "we left something on your bus this morning."

The feet wriggled out and a man stood up, blinking. He wiped his hands on an oily rag.

"What was it?" he said.

"A pair of pants," said Derek.

"No," said the man. "I haven't seen any pants on this bus. Just the ones people were wearing!"

He shook his head and tossed the oily rag into a box. As it sailed through the air, a leg unfolded from the grubby bundle. A leg with green stains on it.

"There they are!" Janey cried.

"Wow!" said the man."I had no idea that was a pair of pants!"

Derek fished the pants out of the box on the end of a wrench. He held them up to examine them.

"Uh-Oh," he said. "They're worse than ever." Janey sighed.

"There's only one thing to do now," she said.

"What's that?"

"We'll have to confess."

On Monday, Derek and Janey got to school early. They slipped into the classroom and took the pants out of the bag.

They saw the oil from the bus and the dirt from Derek's garden. They saw the glue and the green paint. They looked at each other and sighed.

"We have to do it," said Janey. "We have to tell the truth."

Then they put the pants back on the hanger and went off to look for Mr. Such.

They found him in the hall.

"Janey, Derek," said Mr. Such with a smile. "What's all this?"

"It's your suit, Mr. Such," Janey said bravely. "We've got something to tell you."

But before she could say another word, Mrs. Venn burst into the room and grabbed Mr. Such by his arm.

"Fries! Fries!" she screamed.

"No thank you, Mrs. Venn," said Mr. Such. "It's too early in the morning for French fries."

"No, no, Mr. Such. The fries in the kitchen! They're on fire!"

"What?"

Mr. Such hurried over to the kitchen doors and pushed them open. A cloud of blue smoke rolled into the hall.

"My word!" he said, and backed away again.

"Throw some water on it, sir!" squeaked Derek.

"You can't do that," said Mr. Such. "Water will make it worse. I need a cloth or something to smother the flames."

Then he saw the suit dangling on its hanger from Janey's finger.

"I think there's only one thing to do,
Mr. Such," said Janey, and Mr. Such
grabbed the suit.

Of course, the suit was ruined. It
turned into a mangled mess of smoke
and grease. Janey tried to tell Mr. Such
about the green stains and how they
tried to clean them off. But Mr. Such
didn't really listen.

"Never mind," he kept saying.
"Never mind about that."

Mr. Such was the hero of the hour, so he was rather pleased with himself. The principal promised him another brand new suit, and he was pleased with that, too.

"That's great," said Mr. Such. "I can get a nice, bright white one."

"Oh, don't do that," said Janey quickly.

"Why not?"

"Well, we think green would suit you better, don't we, Derek?"

"Much better," Derek nodded. "We think green's a wonderful color."

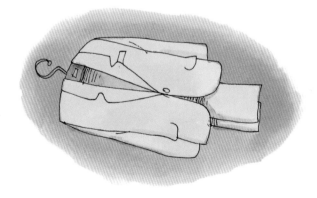

About the author

While I was teaching, I enjoyed drama and reading books aloud with children. This encouraged me to write, and since then I have written a number of scripts for radio, stage and television, around a baker's  dozen or so – that is, thirteen – children's books. I can't ever remember wearing a white suit at school. It would have been asking for trouble.

I enjoy reading, cycling and doing things with my family.